My World

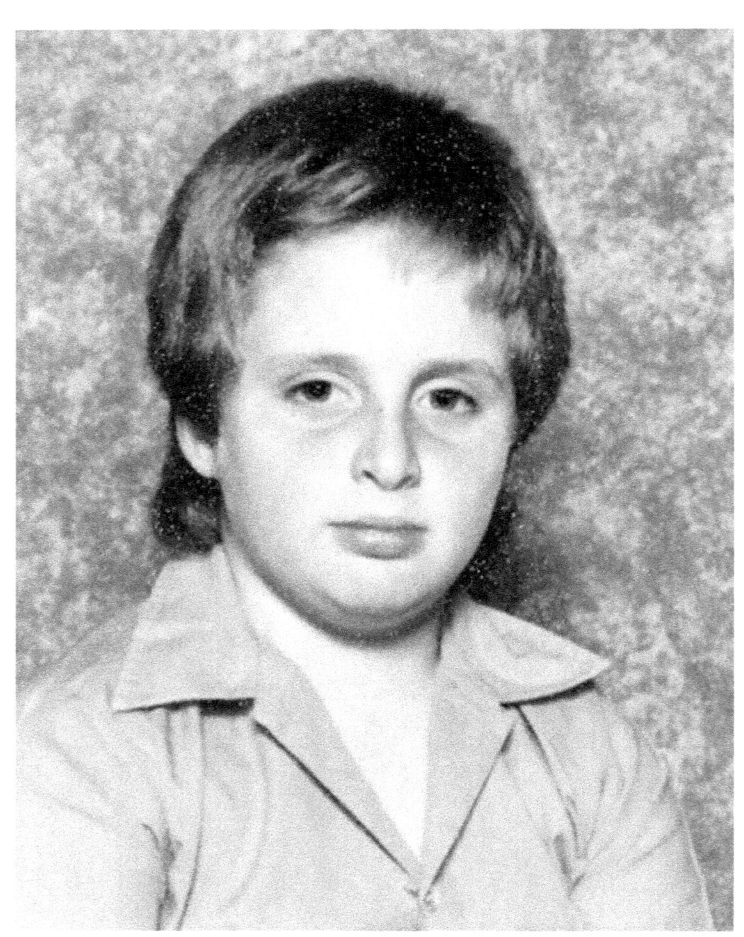

Paul Corfiatis

My World

For everyone who has helped me on life's journey

My World
ISBN 978 1 74027 665 8
Copyright © text Paul Corfiatis 2011
Copyright © cover and internal images Paul Corfiatis 2011

First published 2011
Reprinted 2017

GINNINDERRA PRESS
PO Box 3461 Port Adelaide 5015
www.ginninderrapress.com.au

Contents

Growing Up

The Early Years

The adventure through my eyes and brain has been a roller coaster due to the fact I have autism, a condition which affects the brain and makes you think and behave differently to what a normal person does, but a condition that also gives you supreme talent of creativity and supreme knowledge, even though today I believe I am a normal person because, as you can see, I've written this book all by myself.

My condition is known as high-functioning autism, similar to a person named Temple Grandin who was one of my original major inspirations to write this book, but I don't watch cows like she does. As of today as an adult, I feel so differently to how I did as a child and this book represents the amazing adventure through the 28 or so years of my life, the ups and the downs, and the reactions.

When I was diagnosed with severe autism as a little child, my mum didn't even understand at the time what that condition was, and many people thought I might never ever speak again, but now I speak like a normal person, and even one of my ex-girlfriends didn't believe me when I told her I had this condition. But of course there are differences such as lack of eye contact, a thing I've always struggled with when having a conversation, and the fear of rejection through anxiety.

We travel back to the mid 1980s, an era of Atari 2600s and Commodore 64s, which were the most advanced computers then, and cars which were all new, shiny and hi-tech at that time, but many as of today are old and faded pieces of scrap rattling around on the road. That's long before the days of the Internet, with its websites such as Facebook and Myspace, and before mobile phones…where it all began when I was a little guy.

From the earliest days I can remember lying in my bed and dad holding a blue Sesame Street puppet above my head, with me responding by repeating 'Cookie'…even though it was Grover.

I can also remember from long ago lying in bed as a two-year-old all night long, awake; never remembering if I ever slept, and Mum bringing in a hot milk.

When I was three or four years old I went to kindergarten and when I first saw ceiling fans it really freaked me out, especially when they were running. Because of the unusual motion I used to start crying in vain for teachers to turn them off, but they wouldn't because of the summer and early autumn heat, which didn't bother me so much but certainly bothered other people. The reason why I cried like some crazy boy is because the blades were held on by screws and I used to be worried that the blades would get loose and fall off, chopping off somebody's head or going through and breaking a window. A lot of the time I just tried my hardest not to look at them. I remember one night, as a grown up, I removed the blades from the ceiling fan in my bedroom to clean them in the sink since they were filthy. I thought back to the past. When the fans were turned off I was fine and at other times I was fascinated with them despite all of that. So my support teachers tried to make me not scared of the fans and recover from the fear…and I had no choice.

At the Autistic Children's Centre in Adelaide I used to spend months in a room with a ceiling exhaust bathroom steam-sucking fan which was mounted on a piece of wood. Every hour for ten minutes they used to turn off this fan and I was not very calm, but after a month I didn't used to cry as much. But no doubt that was torture for me at first. To be honest, I hate the word cry but I'm using it in here to make sense…but now back to the story.

A guy name Tim (who I remember was a cameraman) came around to our house in Marion and did a two-hour recording of the kitchen fan above the stove and he played Arabic (Middle Eastern) music in the recording and an electric drill, hair dryer or whatever (I can't really remember) was turned on to make the fan sound noisy (the music that my dad liked because he was originally from Iraq) and after eight weeks or so I was recovered from the fan and I knew it was safe and not deadly and was designed to pump air in some circumstances, and eventually I started to find the fans quite relaxing due to their spinning motion.

I used to like water and drain holes. I used to really like watching water flowing down a drain hole or flushing in the toilet. I used to like the sound and the pattern of the splashing water. Every time me and my mother would go and visit somebody else's house I would go and inspect all their drain holes, run their taps and watch the water flow down the drain holes, and flush all the toilets. I would make my own drain holes in a sandpit by digging a deep hole and burying a pipe or some tube in the ground and flushing water into it, to see how full I could get it.

I used to love going down to the beach in the summer and spend hours digging holes in the sand. I would go and fill a bucket with water and come back and pour water in the hole to see how the pattern of water flow would look. And sometimes, my brother Joe would bash, bury and destroy my drain holes, which made me very upset.

Watching water flow and the patterns it created were very relaxing but people didn't like it because in Adelaide water doesn't come for free.

Other things I was scared off in my early years were noisy lawnmowers. Also the noisy old class 300 and 400 Red Hen railcars, which operated in suburban Adelaide up till late 1996, freaked me out when I first went on them. They rarely operated single railcar Red Hens but we were unlucky to go in a single railcar Red Hen one day and I was astounded. It was tiny, like a rusty maroon bus on the rails. Their engines made a horrible screeching sound. The doors wouldn't close properly, and when the wheels went over track crossings…click clack click. I used to be worried about weird uncommon trains, though, which weren't joined up correctly (like the Superchook railcars 2301 and 2302 in the middle of a Red Hen set).

I used to like certain types of music like reggae (Bob Marley) because I liked the different sounding percussion like woodblocks, groovy bass lines, congas and so on. I also liked Marley's great echoing voice and it always sounded like he was singing in a big empty indoor arena but it was just a studio recording with reverb added.

Heavily vibrating speaker drivers in radios or certain stereo systems used to scare me as well, but I got used to it after about six months and I grew fascinated in speakers and how they worked. I used to always have the bass down low, which sounded terrible, so the speaker driver wouldn't vibrate (cone excursion) too much. I was worried that the dome-shaped dust cap in the middle of the speaker would spit out, because I thought the dust cap only vibrated, and if it spat out, the speaker would blow up.

I couldn't have imagined how I would've reacted if I saw a modern age subwoofer driver at full excursion back then. But I now know that the dust cap is glued in over the voice coil and the whole cone vibrates and speakers do not explode; they just cut out and go dead if they are used way too heavily (clipping and distortion blow speakers).

In 1987, I did a second year at Kindergarten – this time with a lady named Sue, who was the mother of my future support worker when I was 11 to 13. There were some tough times and she was bossy and annoying from my point of view and I didn't like that because I felt like I was being overpowered by a person. She would not let me dig holes a lot in the sandpit and she used to correct me if I did something wrong, which of course I didn't like! (Because from my point of view it was like she was controlling me or, as I've already said, overpowering me.)

I used to spend some time at kindy but later in the year moved back to the Autistic Children's Centre, where it was fun. I also got my first friend; his name was Phillip. I used to sometimes spend time at his house before going home in his mum's Mini. The Mini (a bit like Mr Bean's, light green with a white roof, but no padlock on the door) was fun to ride in, and I used to always stare at its windscreen wipers in the wet. The patterns the wipers made on the dusty windscreen made me fascinated so I used to replicate that pattern with two 30-centimetre rulers on the dew of my bedroom during some winter mornings.

Most of the time it was a fun 50-kilometre ride back home in the minibus that belonged to the Autistic Children's Centre. I enjoyed that ride daily and I used to like the different whining sounds of the engine and gearbox every time the gears were changed. We used to go all the way through the hills in the southern suburbs (such as Belair) to drop off people. I was the last one home usually.

After getting brave with fans, I used to also like spinning objects at times and make my own fans out of toys to further train myself. I would usually turn my bike upside down and spin the wheels on it using the pedals or spin the front wheel using my hand. Then I used to just stand there and watch the wheels slow down similar to the way a ceiling fan slows down after switching it off, but the bike wheels would take much longer to slow down.

I'd sometimes attach white clothes pegs to the inner nut of the wheel to imagine it was fan blades because I used to like the motion of the pegs as the wheel spun around and one of the pegs would be slightly out of alignment vertically, as you would notice on many fans. For my once fear in ceiling fans all of a sudden had become a relaxing motion to watch…a bit like water flowing…and it was even more relaxing watching the fan wobble caused by out of alignment blades or imbalance in weight in the blades.

As an adult I still find this fascinating but today I try my best to be as normal as everyone and I've learnt a lot of things throughout my years of youth and growing up. It has been a long journey, almost the length of a single year on Saturn. Think of it, the journey I've been through has been amazing, the highs and the lows. But life can still be a real disappointment and hit me in the face sometimes.

Reactions

During my childhood years, certain things could scare me, and make me get angry or stressed; to some degree they still do today. Examples include somebody's fist coming towards me; it will make me get distressed and angry. My brother does that to me sometimes, just being silly, and every time I see something coming for my face my head turns around or I try to move my head out of the way fast. My eyes also automatically close. It's just a natural reaction I cannot help.

Also, any loud noises I don't expect like balloons bursting and dogs barking, cars backfiring…but now I'm more prepared about unexpected noises. Whenever I see a person approaching me with a balloon or a balloon tied up against a certain surface like a rough brick wall at a party, I start to worry that the balloon will burst in unexpected fashion, especially if it's moving or getting blown around.

If a small child is carrying one in their hands and pressing on it with their hands, it used to make me put my fingers in my ears no matter where I was, out in public, anywhere, but now I don't do that because I'm more aware. But I still get a bit worried because I'm not quite sure when to expect a potential burst, where it could burst now, or it could burst anytime, creating a loud bang right in my face.

I accidentally popped a beach ball when I was drawing on it with a pen. It scared the living daylights out of me and I started to realise that any item that had compressed air inside could explode or rupture. I don't know when it will burst and it's hard for my brain to figure out things. It still is now. I just try to act normal, but the anxiety starts to kick in with those thoughts in those situations. So sometimes I block my ears or try to get out of the room until I hear a bang, then I slowly walk back in hoping there are no more balloons.

When I was seventeen, I remember at youth group one night we were playing some fun games in the hall and one of the games was something to do with balloons. It got me so scared I ran out and just watched behind the fairly soundproof doors, feeling pretty happy I got out of there. I wouldn't go back in until all the balloons were gone. If somebody snuck up behind me and deliberately burst a balloon, I would jump (not really jumping up and down) and turn around and tell that kid to not do it again, but today I'd probably laugh in fright or get a surprise, probably saying something like 'You bloody scared the heck out of me!' with perhaps a few profanities thrown in there. But if the same thing happened to me when I was about eight or nine years old I'd probably get angry, aggressive and violent and would try to hurt the occupant who burst the balloon because I felt like I was getting overpowered and teased.

My brain tends to think that I'm the boss and I don't know why I'm like this. I can handle these situations much better today. I'm also frightened of certain noises such as dogs barking, which I still don't like at times. A barking dog would make me feel like I was getting told off and make me feel angry and unwelcome and produces anxiety within myself.

When I was younger I used to block my ears whenever we walked by a house that had a high fence. I remember I was walking past somebody's house a few years ago. It had no fence around it, and this dog came charging out barking at me like crazy. One of the owners was out the front of their home. It scared me so much that I got angry and started abusing the owner, feeling like I was overpowered by the dog, so I felt like overpowering the owners back. It didn't feel nice because I was worried that dog was going to attack me. But this time I handled the situation much better. The owner was screaming to call his dog back but the dog just stopped and stood there, after I told it to sit down. I was never going to go near that house again but a few years later I did, and I was on the other side of the road, and that same dog came charging out at me. And more recently, when I was walking home from town with a bag of blank CDs I walked past this house… there appeared that dog (a Labrador), barking at me, thinking I had food in the bag but the dog was now very old and barely walking.

We know a few people who have dogs that spend long terms indoors. But I know that those dogs will only sniff you for a few seconds and go back to their resting spots. So I can handle them much better today, and that was the case when I was going for a walk in July 2006. A fat, uninspiring, shonky-looking man had two small dogs which seemed harmless but the dogs tried attacking me. I told him to walk them on a lead, but he got real nasty. One of the dogs tried to bite my ankle and I kicked it, and the owner whacked me around the back of my neck with a large stick (which didn't hurt that much) and said he would burn down my house (which I didn't believe) but I kept my cool and did not chuck any tantrum like I would have five or ten years earlier.

I found out that these dogs are unregistered. The guy drove an odd-looking van full of stickers and there are rumours that he has been causing trouble with others. The dogs had another go at me, but I told them to sit and they didn't come any closer to me then a metre. There hasn't been any more trouble because the guy moved away from the town I live in. Sometimes I still see him but just keep my distance.

One day I was walking down the street minding my own business and suddenly these dogs angrily started barking at me from inside a van and then I realised how stupid I felt. If I walk past a house and if I see a dog resting on the front porch, I know it's going to come near me and bark at me, but if I see it first that doesn't scare me too much. Or if the dog sees me from fifty metres away and begins barking I'm fine. But if a dog suddenly appeared and started barking when I wasn't expecting it, that would scare me a quite a bit. When I was little it would scare me so bad that I would scream back at the dog, then sort of cry and get distressed afterwards.

Also when I was younger I used to be scared of the dark. If there was loud music being played in a dark room, I wasn't so scared, but if the room was quiet I used to get very frightened, because I couldn't see where I was going, for example, or somebody or something strange would pounce, because it was hard to tell. I used to get out or turn on the light as fast as I could. I used to sleep in a room with a low wattage lamp turned on, or the hallway light turned on.

I remember one night when I was a very young toddler about two or three years old, I was lying awake, and lights from a car came in through the air vent as shadows above my bed, because I was so used to seeing the shadows from the hallway light through the adjacent air vent in the room. That really scared me and I got up and hid behind the curtain and was very frightened. Mum came in and took me into her room.

Today I'm hardly scared of the dark, but I still sleep with a faint light on; but odd noises, such as mosquitoes buzzing, freak me to death almost and a fan, ceiling or desk, is often switched on especially during the summer.

I sometimes go for walks on a dark moonless night to look up at the stars, and you can imagine all those other solar systems and all those unknown extra-solar planets. But sometimes I could hear quite unexpected noises (like night creatures). It can frighten me and can make me feel like leaving the beach. Once the moon comes up (depending on the phase), things are fine, and it's a saying of 'let there be light' from the moonlight, where the sun's light reflects off the surface of the moon back to earth.

I've been playing basketball ever since I was fourteen. I struggled a lot with the pressure in my teen years and suffered from the fear of losing. Despite that, I was a very competitive player in my high school years, but around 2002 I started to accept that both winning and losing are part of the game. I concentrated more on my job and playing hard and it's all been good ever since then.

I played for Special Olympics from 1997 to 1999 and I did not enjoy it because the skills of the players were at times terrible and I am much better off playing with the A-grade local rosters. Watching some of my favourite sporting teams lose can be a bit hard, since I still take it very seriously…such as my favourite AFL team the Adelaide Crows, who are notorious for losing close games, and I still blame them for every loss.

My mum used to always worry about me getting injured in basketball but all the time I had played I never suffered a major injury in ten years of basketball, until in the final game of 2005 I badly sprained my right knee when I landed awkwardly after taking a jump shot. My knee bent inwards and I felt a pop. It scared the heck out of me, not so much hurt me. I managed to walk off the court and the injury wasn't serious. I realised that I had injured the medial ligament in my right knee so it was the best-case scenario. But it surely hurt the following day and I was limping around for a few weeks before I could walk more smoothly because my leg was so stiff. I could hardly bend the knee. It was much better after about eight weeks.

I didn't play basketball in the second half of 2006 because I wasn't feeling very good due to a very long cold winter and I had some asthma problems and suffered a lot from coughing. I went on medication for a couple of months and over the very decent summer I recovered to the way I was before. In 2007 I tried to work on my fitness to get back to playing basketball once again…that includes losing some weight that I gained (a few kilograms) in 2006. In 2008 I was ready to roll again and played a (terrible) game in 2009 in the Devonport B-grade local roster, but I still find A-grade easier because of the better teamwork skills of the players.

I'm hoping to play locally until well into my thirties but that depends on other things in life.

Ups & Downs At School

Most of the time I hated school due to the fear of been overpowered. Back in 1988 I began school and I went to Christ the King School, a Catholic school a few kilometres from our home in Marion, a major suburb of south-west Adelaide. Warradale was the suburb this school was located in.

I was very scared at first, but as soon as I settled into class I did all my work. I had a good first week but my first confrontation with the principal was a nightmarish experience. I got out of class and mucked around in the boys' toilets, watching all the water patterns and flushing them because I wasn't interested in work. I deliberately blocked one toilet and filled it with water to see what things looked like, and a few weeks later I got caught (or dobbed in, as the kids would say). I didn't lie and was banned from using the toilets on my own for the rest of the term. If I needed to go I had to have a teacher come with me under supervision. I was banned at other times over the next three terms.

I used to think it was unfair when my mum gave me packed lunch and other friends got ordered lunch such as pies, sausage rolls, nuggets, burgers and so on. But my mum would let me have hot lunch once a week and I really enjoyed it. But I missed out on it, and I used to look in the bins for any uneaten food, especially fresh food in paper bags which had been wasted and dumped in the bins. I used to take it out, wash it under a tap and eat it (as of now, yuck!). I just didn't like healthy food but luckily that has all changed today. After a few months I stopped doing that because I thought it was stupid…really stupid.

Once we were writing words in our books of the blackboard and I was in a silly mood that day. I was supposed to write 'ship' but I wrote the word 'shit' on purpose to see how the teacher would react and oh boy didn't she go bananas! But I modified the T and changed it into a P.

I also went on a school camp that year and I found it difficult at times. I don't remember where we went to but I enjoyed it for most of the time, but at other times I felt like I wanted to go home and see Mum. There was a bonfire and I just stared at it and ignored the instructor, though some of the teachers would help me like do up my shoelaces and so on.

Grade 1 (my second year) was more fun, with a better teacher. Despite the toilet banning troubles, I did enjoy the whole year. If I got silly and upset, the teacher used to sit me down in a quiet room for five minutes to try to calm me down.

But I used to be interested in the human body, space (astronomy) and dinosaurs and the prehistoric world. Instead of doing current work, I used to draw lots of pictures of these subjects, especially human reproduction, which to the teacher was rude (at least I had self-taught sex education long before others). So I was banned from doing that, but from my point of view it was not rude but interesting.

Grade 2 was with the same teacher in the same class and was a better year than Grade 1 for the first three years. But in the fourth term our teacher had a severe illness (which she survived) and a new relief teacher replaced her. Well, it was a very tough, frustrating time, and once this relief teacher even threw me against a wall and hurt me. It wasn't too painful but more scary and agonising and it got so awful and stressful. One day when the pressure and stress got too much, I ran away from the school and walked home. But I was too scared to go into our house because I was worried that my dad would yell at me and because I did not cope well being yelled at, the fear of being overpowered was frightening.

The relief principal found me and he took me back to the school. He didn't get angry at me but I was very frightened he would. He sat me down in the office until school ended and I was allowed to go home.

The last few weeks of the fourth term were actually much better and the teacher felt sorry for me a lot of the time.

In the upstairs classrooms there were ceiling fans but I wasn't too scared of them any more and I actually liked staring at them spinning around. I used to stare at their motion all the time, and it would stop me from doing work.

In 1991 I moved into Grade 3 and the work was getting harder and more interesting (and frustrating at times). I was in another classroom with another teacher who was an elderly teacher in her 60s (now retired). We had to write in our Dear Journal books every Monday and I used to make up stories most of the time because on the weekends we didn't do much. Using pens was banned and we had to use lead pencils until we got our pen licence, a system that I didn't like.

Later in the year the teacher went overseas for a holiday and we got another relief teacher; the best of the worst. She was a bully to everyone in the classroom, especially me and my best friend back then; his name was Stephen. I also had another friend named Stephen, and he had autism, and he was having hell. She was an inexperienced teacher; most of us in the classroom didn't do much work. She left the school after a couple of weeks and another more experienced relief teacher took over. I always hated her because of her loud voice but she was a good guitarist.

Our Grade 3 teacher came back later in the year after her holiday in England and Wales and I was good again and enjoyed the rest of the year.

Grade 4 was a good year. I did most of my work and that year we got homework to do. I didn't do it because it was too hard for me, and I found it really hard to figure out what to do. I used to think home was home, and I used to be thinking homework is school at home, but home wasn't school. The teacher understood my problems and difficulties and I never really got into bad trouble for that.

That year we got computers into our classes, old-fashioned Apple II computers, which have black and green displays only and 5.25 external floppy disk drives. There was a horse racing game I enjoyed playing a lot to see how much money I'd win. There was a solar system simulator program I really liked because I was interested in space and used to enjoy making my own solar systems, and used to like the way the planets orbited their stars. It also helped me understand about gravity. For example, a planet closer to the sun orbits at a greater speed than a planet further out.

Grade 5 didn't go well. The teachers were bullies. I used to be annoyed a lot by this girl named Jane, and for all the years she called me Paul Peppermint Plaps. Wow, what a name!

One day while sitting at the table in class, the principal was there watching and I was doing absolutely nothing, and I just moved my hand to scratch my head. She took me down to her office and threatened to call the police on me. I was expelled from school for the rest of the year, two weeks after.

I figured out the principal was just a plain bully. She accused me of sexually abusing Jane. My parents went to court later in the year for this. After being expelled from school I felt very happy that it was all over! Later in the year, me and about fifty or sixty great friends got a big party together and we went to a barbecue. Me and another autistic boy named Stephen made a steam machine by throwing water on a hotplate barbecue surface.

I still know quite a few of those friends; on a recent trip in March 2003 I saw them all, and with the introduction of Facebook many have found me.

I had to do homework, which was sent by mail, at home in my bedroom, and I really enjoyed it. It was much more of a pleasure without the students and the teachers. Later on I went to Marion Primary School, a nearby school in our suburb. I spent the last few weeks of Grade 5 there.

In Grade 6 I was in a special class where there were students with learning problems. The students in this small class were Isaac, Michael, Sharlene, Andrew and me. Isaac left midway through the year. The teacher, Mr Broadway, could play the guitar (but only in a basic way) and I learned to play the guitar by watching his hands. Now I can play fast flamenco and so on.

I did my work very well that year and it was very enjoyable. In August I suffered a fractured wrist after two heavy falls off my bike and I got it plastered up with solid fibreglass tape, which formed a cast. The bad news was that it was my right hand, and I was worried I couldn't do my schoolwork and not get points, because my work was going to be messy with my left hand. But somehow I achieved something few achieve. I could actually write with my right hand and I had a great term; maybe the best in my schooling life. Since we had this points system, I used to try to get as many points as I could; sometimes as many as forty. In the fourth term the points system stopped but I still worked hard.

When the fibreglass cast came off my arm, it still felt a bit sore, and I strengthened it back up by dribbling a basketball, and I started to like basketball.

At the end of the year David Broadway announced he was going to move on. We sort of missed him, but that's life. Michael went on to high school and Sharlene and I were the only ones remaining. We continued on Grade 7 the next year in different classes, but we were good friends and still are today.

Grade 7 was with a normal class (Grades 6 and 7 mixed together) and I had a little trouble, but the teacher named Jennifer was a pretty nice teacher and understood my difficulties. I did most of my work that year, and being 13 years of age I started to get interested at the girls a bit; and there were more girls than boys in the class.

I made some good new friends; one of them was a dude named Leigh. We used to have fun playing on the SNES at home on the weekends, mainly one on one with Mortal Kombat II. It was a fun game and I liked playing as the fighters Scorpion, Sub Zero, Rayden, Lui Kang and Kung Lao.

In August we went on a school camp to Mannum near the Murray River. It was lots of fun and I really had a great time. It was very interesting as well. We slept in small material rooms, separated from each other, which could hold four people each. One girl I used to be fixated on was Sarah, because her hobby was like mine, collecting (expensive) trading cards, which was a big thing then. I still have all those cards now plus more. We used to swap, sell and buy them in secret private meetings out of class during lunchtime.

Another good friend was Nick, a big strong boy who looked like a rugby player, who I used to like playing basketball with. He had a mean-looking face but wasn't really a mean person.

There was a blonde girl I used to be fixated on named Courtney; she was a small shy and quiet person at that time. I wasn't a huge friend of hers.

Later in the year we moved to Ulverstone, Tasmania, and the whole class put up a big farewell party. Lots of fun. I got lots of cards and big hugs from everybody. Even that shy girl named Courtney actually kissed me on my left cheek (wow!), something I didn't expect her to do.

I would spend the last month of grade 7 at Ulverstone High School before doing Grades 8, 9 and 10 there.

In 1996 I played basketball for the U15s roster in Ulverstone when I played in my first game. It was scary and I was pretty shy. I did score a clutch basket late in the game for my only points of the game, though, which got us to within one. We almost came back from 20 down to win, but lost by three points. We would lose five of our next six games before winning our last eight including the grand final. As the season went on, I got more confident and became a good defender, since I was the biggest guy on the court when I was 14, but unfortunately I got outgrown by many later on. I wasn't a great scorer, though. One thing that got me frustrated was that if the scores were tied we would not play overtime.

I played basketball up to 1999 and improved very well, but at times it got frustrating – especially some of the losses. I spent 2000 off but played more basketball in 2001 and 2002, both on losing teams, and I played better overall; but in 2003 other things took me away from it.

Now back to school. I began Grade 8 and I spent a lot of the time in the special class. It was actually good fun. The teacher's name was Leigh (yes, another Leigh) and he was always very nice and helpful.

1996 was the year of the Atlanta Olympic Games so our class had our own Olympic Games; not really sports, but mainly card games, board games. It was fun and I won a few medals. I won a gold medal in table soccer/hockey. Two small nets were placed on the table and you had to try to bang a golf ball into the net using a ruler. It was hard to score and the first one to score two goals won.

During free time I used to spend a lot of my time writing on the computers. I also got to use the Internet that year during times. But at other times I used to be with my normal Grade 8 class. There were a nice bunch in that class but a few of the boys acted silly.

I found science and chemistry very interesting. When I was little I used to be interested in the human body, reproduction and the human embryo, microscopes, history and geology of the earth and space. But we did a lot of chemistry and experiments with acids, like putting zinc into hydrochloric acid and making chemical reactions occur, or boiling liquids in round glass containers under Bunsen burners to create gases. I always had a fascination with bubbling liquids and used to stare at the bubbles in the boiling liquids.

In Grade 9 and 10 I had to leave Mr Bird's class and I started getting into the girls a bit more then, but was too shy and worried about them, and I wouldn't say much to them. I did get a support worker that year. Out of school I was on a Tasmanian basketball team that went off to Newcastle, NSW, in July, but we didn't win any games. It was frustrating but a good learning experience.

In my last two years of Ulverstone High School, Grades 9 and 10, I did a few interesting subjects. I did cooking (food) art, and more science. I spent times with Mr Bird and would usually have lunch in his room.

Science was my favourite subject at high school. We did an experiment with liquid nitrogen at a temperature of 196 centigrade. We would put water into it and make these weird structures of ice, and the water was frozen as hard as rock and would take ages to melt. Every time something at room temperature was put in the liquid nitrogen the nitrogen would boil so we had to wear gloves, face masks and goggles to prevent any of the cold vapour getting into our faces. We also made liquid nitrogen bombs, where we poured the liquid nitrogen into a two-litre Coke bottle and sealed the lid. As it evaporated, the pressure inside the bottle built up, and 'bang'…what a loud noise even from one hundred metres away.

I also did art and did some good drawings of space and planets. The school even brought one of my drawings for $50 dollars.

Towards the end of Grade 10 we had a leavers' dinner and I had to wear a suit and tie, and I resembled the fictional Borat character from Kazakhstan. I thought I looked pretty silly, but others liked me more. I didn't really like leavers' dinner very much, in fact. I also didn't like the meal; you got what you got, and you couldn't ask for what you wanted, which I thought was bad.

I spent four months or so at Don College in Devonport during

1999 before moving to Hellyer College in Burnie. I did Grade 11 (1999) and 12 (2000) part-time, and had two different casual girlfriends throughout Grade 12. The reason I went part-time was because the difficulties I have to cope with. I was always with a support worker; his name was Steve and he's no longer a worker, but one of my best friends still.

Then I was writing music on the computer, midi files and producing my own compositions, as I try to get an album out of my best music. In 2001, I started working at Total Audio Productions. I still use this recording studio today, and have improved vastly since I first went there.

I returned to Don College Tasmanian Academy in 2010 for art classes twice a week and it has been challenging but enjoyable at the same time.

Interests, Achievements & Goals

My Predictive Scientific Mind

I've had many different interests in my life, mainly scientific subjects like the human body, astronomy, microscopes, and also cars, artwork, and music.

I taught myself sex education, as in my early childhood I used to be very interested in the human body and how it worked, and the shape of the human embryo and how a baby is created. I used to spend hours drawing pictures of the embryo and body parts on paper. I used to be interested in reproduction and how a new human being is created and was interested in comparing it to other animals. I used to always write handmade books which showed cut-away diagrams. It was incredible – as a strange alien object would eventually convert itself into a living, thinking person – just like me.

I used to draw lots of pictures of space and planets when I was young and I still do it sometimes. I have also done some artwork of worlds beyond our imagination, using kindergarten paints, not oil paints, and various different sizes of paintbrushes. I started painting pictures of planets in Grades 2 and 3 but thought I wasn't that good. A couple of space art books encouraged me and inspired me. In Grades 9 and 10 at Ulverstone High School when I had art, I used to complete good paintings within just two hours of non-stop work! All the paintings were based on fictional extra-solar planets out of our solar system.

I used to be good at doing light shading and gradients, thus painting pictures of crescent planets, and the distant sun providing the light for the crescent shape. The distant stars were dotted on using a liquid paper pen, but due to the roundness of the actual planet's dark side I could not dot stars on that region.

I used to also do moons of the planets in some of these paintings, thus creating a smaller and more nearby crescent transiting in front of its parent planet. I like realism and from my point of view everything must be as accurate as possible. One painting I did in Grade 10 was a spaceship flying in front of a planetary backdrop, and Ulverstone High School bought that painting for $50 dollars. It's the first item I sold in my life. It is now framed somewhere in the school.

I also did another painting seen from the moon of a gas giant planet, and all the hills and surface, using the correct shading technique with the lighter side pointing the main nearby star.

Today I'm still fascinated in space and astronomy. I always read books about it, or surf the net about it when I'm bored. The planets that interest me the most are gas giants such as Jupiter, the largest planet in the solar system, with its various coloured bands and eddies and the great red spot.

I wonder what an extra-solar planet, five times the mass of Jupiter, would look like. Well, first, despite being five times more massive than Jupiter, it would be a similar size (perhaps smaller) to Jupiter, but its surface gravity would be five times stronger than Jupiter's, so more pressure crushing in on the inner region of the core, so its core would be much hotter than Jupiter's. But the planet is the same size – so the atmosphere would have to have extremely dramatic active cloud circulation, and the cloud features would be smaller, but more active, like thin wavy lines of spaghetti or noodles.

I believe that nearly every star would have planets around it; certain stars may have life on one of their planets and I believe that life is common throughout the galaxy; but an advanced civilisation like ours is rare, because the creatures on many of these so-called undiscovered Earth-like worlds are not as intelligent as mankind, or have not evolved as much as the life on our planet has today.

Stars more massive than the sun, like Sirius, are hotter and brighter, and live shorter lives, but cooler stars, known as red dwarfs like Proxima Centauri or Barnard's Star, live much longer lives than the sun. Sun-like stars are the ones more likely to have habitable planets but a lot of the gas giants discovered so far around other sun-like stars orbit extremely close to their stars – much closer in than Mercury, and therefore many would be larger than Jupiter in apparent size, due to the higher concentrations of heat bloating up their atmospheres. They could be huge rocky planets that formed nearby, or gas giants that migrated inward from a further region, sending other closer inter-terrestrial planets into deep space or unstable orbit, or crashing them into their star, erasing the possibility of life.

If Jupiter migrated inwards millions of years ago, our planet would have been either sent into deep space out of our solar system into an endless trek in between the stars, captured into orbit around Jupiter (making it a moon) or thrown into another direction, sending it into a highly unstable orbit or into the fiery globe sun, to disappear forever within the inferno.

More massive stars like the sun have so much material that it creates a body massive enough to become a second star, thus making a binary star system, or double star system. But other single stars like Epsilon Eridani have solar systems similar to our own. In 2000, a Jupiter mass planet was found orbiting the star, which is a bit cooler and less massive than the sun. It was orbiting at a distance equivalent to about halfway between Mars and Jupiter, so further inward may be terrestrial planets, and maybe one with liquid water on its surface.

If an Earth-sized planet is too close in, the water vaporises due to the heat and produces inferno-like conditions, called a runaway greenhouse effect. The planet Venus in our solar system is the hottest planet; it is shrouded in an atmosphere of carbon dioxide, and sulphuric acid clouds with a surface pressure of 90 times that of Earth; you would be crushed, burnt and instantly killed by the dense supercritical atmosphere.

A piece of paper on Venus would burn into smoke, and dissolve into the supercritical fluid air, since the pressure of the carbon dioxide gas is above its critical point on Venus. If a planet at the distance of

Venus had a day of 15 hours long, there would be way less chance of it becoming an inferno. Venus rotates very slowly, every 243 days, and it rotates clockwise, the backwards or retrograde direction, and its day is longer than its year.

If Earth rotated every 243 days, instead of 24 hours, there would be a huge heat build-up during the day in which the oceans would start to evaporate and cause a runaway greenhouse effect, and eventually the Earth would become like Venus. If the Earth was placed too far out, like at Mars or Jupiter's place, the less heat would cause the oceans to freeze and the Earth's oceans would be frozen and look bright white. We might still be able to live here; but not for long – the plants would freeze to death and the food supply for humans would go, and we would freeze and starve to death after about twenty or so years. The number one rule to survival is to eat it natural, not mechanical, and all animals eat other living things, plant or animal, except for earthworms, who eat dirt and soil.

At times I also like looking at the night sky and watching moonrises, no matter what phase. I will go down to the beach, even in the early hours of the morning, to watch a moonrise on a clear night. I also like looking for the thin crescent moon in the morning and evening twilight, especially when it's difficult to see, and very young or old (within a day of new moon). The youngest moon I have ever spotted with my eyes was 21 hours old.

To most people, the rising moon appears huge when on the horizon but I did this experiment. I used a ruler to measure the actual width of the moon, by holding the ruler at arm's length directly in front of my face; a rising moon (on the ocean horizon) for example is 0.6 to 0.8 centimetres, while the moon appears roughly the same size when it is up high in the sky, maybe slightly larger at 0.8 to one centimetre. There is no doubt that a moonrise is a spectacular event, with its gold/orange and even red colour. A rising full moon appears squashed due to atmospheric interaction.

I used to be interested in dinosaurs when I was a kid, especially the gigantic brontosaurus or the deadly Tyrannosaurus rex. Then I started wondering, did the Earth look different all those millions of years ago? So I started reading books about the Earth and its geology, and it showed maps of the Earth as it is believed it looked like. About 220 million years ago, the Earth was believed to be covered in one huge super continent which scientists named Pangaea.

I then learned about what was causing continental drift. It was caused by activity inside our planet. Volcanoes and earthquakes are a part of all this. We live on an active planet – its surface is teaming with life, oceans, just about everything a planet's gravity can make things do. And inside is also very active.

The surfaces of Venus and Mars have remained unchanged for millions of years. I believe that the light tidal-tugging caused by the moon heats up the interior of our planet, because the moon is 3,476 kilometres in diameter compared to the Earth's 12,768 kilometres in diameter. Our moon is quite large for the size of the planet it orbits, compared to the four big moons of Jupiter. Jupiter is roughly 11 times bigger than Earth, while Io is roughly the same size as our moon; Europa is slightly smaller, Ganymede and Callisto are slightly bigger (and smaller than Mercury). The innermost of Jupiter's big moons has heavy volcanic activity caused by tidal forces 10,000 times stronger than the Moon on the Earth; so Io is always resurfacing itself, because there are about eight to ten active volcanoes erupting at an extremely violent rate, and hotter then Earth's volcanoes. Its surface is covered by quantities of sulphur caused by these eruptions, causing it to be many different colours, like white, yellow, orange, red, brown and black. White areas are the coldest regions and black areas are the hottest.

Other planets like Venus and Mars are less active in their interiors (especially Mars). Venus is an inferno as explained before; we are not quite sure if there are any active volcanoes on its surface at present days. Scanned images from a 1990s Magellan probe revealed thousands of volcanoes on its fry-pan hot surface.

There are also dead volcanoes on Mars, including Olympus Mons. A volcano five times higher than Mt Everest pokes out of the Martian atmosphere and is several hundred kilometres wide. But Mars is a dead world, no activity on its surface for millions of years. The moon has also not changed for millions of years too, and its interior isn't hot enough for active volcanoes.

Both Venus and Mars don't have any big moons. Mars has two rocks in orbit, the size of a city, Phobos and Deimos, which would look like very bright stars in the night sky and they have no effect on the planet, while Venus has no moons as we know.

Mercury, the innermost planet to the sun, is a cratered world in between the sizes of Mars and the moon; it has been dead for millions of years. Any atmosphere has been vaporised into space by the intense heat of the sun. At noon on the equator the temperature on Mercury is about 400 degrees Celsius, while at night it drops to minus 90 Celsius; the polar regions of Mercury would be about minus 80 degrees Celsius, so there may be a chance for ice to exist there.

One day I'd like to write a book about space, and planets. I have always had a good knowledge of space and astronomy.

I also like observing the moon and looking at our satellite through binoculars, which show craters, hills and whatsoever. Some nights I will stay up very late to watch the moon rise, like when its in last quarter for example. Some other nights I will walk down to the beach to watch a moonrise on a very clear night, such as a moonrise a few days after full moon.

One very clear morning, about 45 minutes before sunrise, I looked out my window and saw an extremely thin crescent moon, 27 days old (the moon takes around 28 days to orbit the Earth). At first I saw the dark Earth-lit side over a house, and I knew that was the moon.

A few months before that, I saw a one-day-old very thin crescent moon setting in the twilight; it was so thin and close to the sun in the daytime skies it could not be seen until after sunset. The very thin moon also sets before twilight ends. I always know where the moon is, what time I estimate it to rise. On 8 May 2001 the moon was one day after full moon, so it was quite bright.

The wider the moon's phase, the more times you'll be able to see it at night. For example, full moon rises near or just after sunset; first quarter half moon rises at lunchtime and sets about midnight; while the last quarter half moon rises around 11 p.m. to midnight and sets around lunchtime.

So if you look in the right place at the right time you'll be able to see the moon in the daytime sky, especially when its a crescent first or last quarter. The three-day thinnish crescent moon, for example, is located about 35 to 40 degrees east of the sun, while on the opposite end the third last crescent moon can be glimpsed in the daytime sky 35 to 40 degrees west of the sun – so if you look in the right place, you would find it. But the best time to look at crescent moons is just before or just after sunset depending if it's in first or last quarter.

My Thoughts About Extra-terrestrial Life

This is a note I wrote on a Facebook group about extra-solar planets in response to my beliefs about extraterrestrial life.

I believe that every single star not only in the galaxy but in the universe contains planets, and a majority of binary stars also contain planets. Out of my estimates I believe that one in every five single stars of a spectral type between F and K contain a planet between 0.5 and five earth masses in the comfort zone of their system.

Choose 100 of these Earth-like planets, and perhaps five of them contain life on their surfaces, mainly because their rotational periods are between 10 hours and 100 hours. I don't think life can exist on a planet with a very long rotational period because of the extreme changes in temperature.

Take 100 of these worlds with life, including Earth, and it's Earth which is the only world with an advanced civilisation. The 99 other worlds have plant and animal life forms, but do not have the technology that humans possess. I reckon the odds of an advanced civilisation are one in about 100,000 Earth-like worlds. Despite those odds, there could be millions of advanced civilisations in the universe.

Perhaps 500 Earth-like worlds in our galaxy could possess an advanced civilisation. That's extremely rare, given the fact that there are many more planets than stars in our galaxy. Out of those 500 advanced civilisations, intelligent races that have technology and cities, humans may be the most advanced of them all; if not, they will be in the top 10 for sure. Mankind is far more advanced than anything.

On the Right Track

Another thing I used to like were trains. I used to like everything about them. The noise their wheels made, the speed they travelled at, what number the carriages were, their design, the gauge, the tracks they travelled on, and lots more. The width of standard gauge tracks is 1.435 metres, and they are used all over Europe, Australia and the United States; but the widths of the narrow-gauge tracks in Tasmania are 1.067 metres. The tracks the Adelaide suburban trains travelled on were 1.600 metres wide; that is called broad gauge.

When we lived in Adelaide, we used to live near the train tracks and I would spend many hours out the front of our house staring at the trains that used to go past. They were the Trans Adelaide 2000 class jumbo, and 3000 class pox box railcars, and the Red Hen railcars, which were still in service when I was a kid, especially on grand prix days, when they used to operate the Monday to Friday routes on a weekend and many extra routes in between too.

Each train car used to have a number on the side, like 30xx or 31xx, for example 3003 or 3115. If I went on 3115 one day and got on 3115 in two years' time, I would know that was the carriage I sat in two years ago. So I would try to sit in the same seat I sat in, if it was empty.

I also liked high-speed trains like the TGV in France because they are the fastest operating trains in the world. They run on electricity, so they don't cause pollution or anything, just like trams.

I also was interested in steam locomotives for some time and I used to like the wheel arrangements on them and how many wheels they had. I also liked the noise the wheels made when a train moved at speed. That inspired me to start making trains out of milk cartons when I was about 11 or 12. I would stick two milk cartons together and draw doors and windows on it, put a number on it too, and attach wheels (mainly Lego) to the bottom. Then I used to join the trains together and wheel them through the house. Since our house had not much carpet and the floors were mainly polished wood, it used to make a crunching noise, making it sound like a train.

When we moved to Tasmania I lost interest in trains because not many operate here, mainly freight trains, which come through town a few times a day. But we are far from the line anyway.

But there is a tourist train ride service called Don River railway near Devonport. They restore old steam locomotives and run a fifteen-minute ride. The train runs on the usual narrow-gauge tracks used in Tasmania but goes very slowly for people to enjoy the view and to scream out windows, probably no faster than 30 kilometres per hour.

As a child I used to draw lots of pictures of trains, in particular strange high-speed train designs, since it was something I felt like doing to relax me. Another thing I used to do, like most naughty boys, was put small stones on the tracks and, as a train came, it would crush the stones creating a crunching noise.

Zooming In On the Hidden

I used to be interested in microscopes too. My favourite was the scanning electron microscope, a device which allows you to see close up in 3D! The scanning electron microscope can magnify from 5X to 400,000X plus, allowing you to view in 3D very small objects almost invisible to the naked eye.

In 1990 I went to see a scanning electron microscope with my support worker. My mum and brother came along and we had a look at a house fly under the scanning electron microscope in 3D. It's an amazing ability to turn a black flying buzzing object into a real monster with strange eyes and hairy body. The fly close-up in 3D looks like a huge hairy alien with wings and six legs.

Human blood cells look like strange cake-like discs. A cross-section of paper looks like an amazing complex of fibres when seen close up in 3D.

A scanning electron microscope looks far different from an ordinary microscope. Modern scanning electron microscopes are operated by computer and are fairly easy to use, but the older ones I saw when I was a kid were not operated by computer software.

You place the specimen inside the microscope column, which is a cylinder-shaped object about 40 to 80 centimetres tall with a door at the bottom. The specimen of a fly standing on a drawing pin like object is placed inside the microscope column door, and the specimen is covered by a plating of gold vapour or something. The door is closed and sealed, and a vacuum is applied to drop the pressure inside. Then an electron beam is beamed from the top of the column on to a specimen, scanning the surface of the specimen and transmitting it to the computer the user is using. And the person at the computer controls the magnification and specimen; rotating, using the mouse and keyboard.

There are icons where you can rotate the view up or down, left or right, and you drag a selection box on the area where you want to zoom in to. Once you zoom in, it will auto-focus, bringing the sharp 3D view into clear focus. You can zoom out to your previous magnification by pressing the '-' button.

As a child I always wanted to study electron microscopy when I grew up but it never came around to that after our move to a regional area from a mainland city. Even though the interest went away, I'm still fascinated by the imagery that these machines can produce.

Aircraft/Flying

With my interest in vehicles such as cars and trains I suddenly started developing an interested in planes. In 1992 I went on my first flight, which was on a small turboprop aircraft. My uncle and I flew to Kangaroo Island, and we went on the then well- known Australian regional airline named Kendell Airlines. Our plane was a Swedish-built

Saab 340A that was built in 1985. It was a 34- seat plane, and I sat in seat 7C. The seats were covered in white sheepskin. Upon boarding the plane through its retractable staircase, I noticed the words 'City of Mt Gambier' written on the door. The aircraft was mostly white with two black and dark red stripes running down the side of the fuselage, which bottomed out at the rear, and two large four-bladed propellers with one mounted on each wing.

After we got in and fastened our seatbelts the aircraft's turboprop engines started up, then unfeathered, and we taxied out to the city end of the runway at Adelaide Airport, and you could hear the buzz from the props as they spun four times faster than a ceiling fan on top speed.

Once on the runway, the engines sped up to full power and the noise and vibration from the propellers was very noticeable. We flew out over the ocean towards Kangaroo Island on a gloomy and cloudy day, and the whole flight was fairly noisy but not deafening. We landed at Kingscote Airport 40 minutes after we left Adelaide, with the flight mostly over water. The airport on Kangaroo Island was very small with a single runway.

Several days later we returned to Adelaide on a smaller Kendell aircraft which was a Swearighan Metro II 16-seat plane (originally 19 seats, but reconfigured) and I thought it was a bit quieter than the Saab, and was a neat little plane with comfortable seats.

The name 'Kendell' (I actually thought it was hilarious (the 'dell' made me crack up, because of its spelling but I found out that it was someone's last name) started getting me interested in their planes and when they were built. I sent a letter to their main travel agent in Wagga Wagga, NSW, and the managing director sent me many brochures and a T-shirt I always wore to the beach.

Then I started getting interested in other airlines and passenger aircraft. The other two Australian domestic airlines were Qantas and Ansett, until the collapse of Ansett and the introduction of Virgin Blue, Jetstar and Tiger Airways, etc.

I began drawing pictures of those aircraft with my made-up airline on them because I wanted to see something different. I used to make up silly airline names like 'Flying Dolphin or Whale' and used to draw my own design on it, or names like 'Bullet Express' or 'Killer Airways' and so much more. I liked to draw my own airline layout on my favourite passenger aircraft like Concorde and 747s. My favourite one I liked drawing on was the Saab 340.

My interest in aircraft faded for many years but now I like to photograph aircraft in action, and discovered that Burnie–Wynyard airport has some excellent spots for photography. You get Saab 340s coming here too, not Kendell but a current airline named Regional Express, which for several years operated some of the older Kendell aircraft in a different livery or colour scheme. Many of my photos have been uploaded onto the Internet.

I also have some good photos of passenger jet aircraft (mainly Qantas) in Melbourne and Adelaide, as well as a few from my first trip to Helsinki, Finland, in 2005 which probably sparked my interest back into aircraft. I've also taken photos of passenger aircraft from Melbourne and Adelaide.

My trip to Finland in 2005 yielded some spectacular views outside the window. I remember the fiery red twilight and tropical cloud formations before sunrise, about two hours before we landed in Hong Kong when heading north, and another spectacular sunrise over Siberia on our way back from Helsinki.

For many months I had a plan to fly over to Melbourne airport and back on the same day on a regional aircraft from Tasmania. In November 2008, I finally got around to doing it, flying from Burnie to Melbourne and back, and taking photos, and recording videos from outside the window.

The Driving Force

I am also interested in cars. I remember one morning in 1989 or so, I was sitting in the back of the car as Mum went in to get some milk and bread. Every few cars which were shooting by on the highway had the word Mitsubishi written on their rear ends, with the three diamonds beside it of course. I thought that the word sounded hilarious when you said it very fast. It sounded like a malfunctioning Japanese professor. I would get nervous when I was to go in a Mitsubishi car, but that eased away as I grew older.

In March 1999 my support worker Steve and I started going and looking at car yards because I was starting to get interested to learn to drive; and in August I passed my test to get my L plates. I thought it was an astonishing achievement for a person like me recovering from autism. A few weeks later I got into the RAC learning car, a 1997 Ford Laser sedan (which was really a re-badged Mazda). At first I wanted to drive an auto only because it was easier to drive; then I wanted to learn in a manual car so I could drive anything – manual or auto –when I got my P plates.

After a couple of deep breaths, I turned on that 1997 Ford Laser learning car. It took me about four or five tries to get it going, because I kept stalling it by accident…but then I got it going. It shot off very quickly, and my first gear change was shocking; from first to second there was a huge thumping noise. But as every week progressed I got better and better, and by December I was hardly stalling the car; but my take-offs were still a bit poor at times.

On 19 January 2000 I bought my first car and registered it – an old, cheap 1985 Mitsubishi Magna sedan which was manual. It was falling apart but it gave me a good year. Mum and I went out in it every night, and by April I was ready to go for my Ps. Me and the driving instructor went out in my car, and took it for a test run, and I passed the test first try.

Getting my Ps up on the windows of my car was just too much for me. I pretended to look tough and not smile; it was a good day for me and later on in that week I drove from Ulverstone to Campbelltown all by myself before Mum took over from Campbelltown to Hobart. We went for my mum's sister's wedding. I drove all the way back by myself and holding up miles of traffic was sure frustrating.

After selling my car, I used Mum and Dad's car, but in 2004 I bought another cheap Magna, a 1989 model wagon with nice blue paint, because I was in desperate need of a car. It served me well for 20 months, when I traded it in for my current car, a 1996 TE Magna auto (a completely different car). I wanted to get a 1997 Toyota Vienta manual, but I couldn't get the finance for the Toyota, so I ended up getting the Mitsubishi.

After doing some Internet research, the Mitsubishi turned out to be a better buy than the Toyota. It was all paid off within two years and I now own it, and after a few mechanical repairs it's going well, and I'm slowly planning to do it up into the way I like it. The windows have already been tinted and I have added a CD player and better rear speakers – nothing that flash.

Later in 2009 I purchased some 17-inch alloy rims for it. It feels safer to drive with the new wheels and the car certainly looks a lot better as well. Since I'm saving up at home, I decided to keep the car mostly in its stock form, so I won't be doing too many modifications to the engine and exhaust because I believe it goes good enough for me. The car has served me excellently over the years I've owned it and I've driven it on long highway trips endless times.

It's good for the highway with its V6 engine and gets me where I have to go, since there is hardly any public transport in north-west Tasmania. I feel more secure in larger cars, especially for highway driving, even though it's not as big as a Ford Falcon and especially not as big as a Chrysler 300C.

I chose to drive because as I got older I thought it would be unfair for my mum and any possible support workers, and I knew I could do it; it's a big achievement for a person with HFA. If I was still living in Adelaide I might have only used public transport and might not have been driving at all; so improving my independent life by driving has helped take the strain away from others.

Driving is a challenge. That's because other drivers are very impatient and I'm learning to be more patient as time passes by.

Trading Cards

In 1994 my brother Joe started collecting NBA basketball trading cards, which were a popular thing back then (and as you could predict, the emotions between the kids, mainly boys, could run high). I started collecting in about October of 1994 and I have put up a valuable collection of trading cards ever since then, buying mostly packs but single cards too. I didn't swap much at all.

I have NBA basketball cards with popular mid-1990s players like Michael Jordan, Shawn Kemp and Shaquille O'Neal. I also liked the 1994 Australian basketball NBL series made by Futera and I have the full series one and two sets, and nearly all of the rather not that easy to find inserts. An insert card is a special type of card inserted in random amounts of packs. If the odds were 1:40 packs, it is more valuable, but if the odds were 1:5 packs, it would be worth less, depending on the player.

I don't buy cards much any more; maybe once a year I get a box of packs or some single cards in. My huge collection which I still currently have is mainly NBA, Australian NBL and anything Futera, F1, Baseball, a few AFL cards (Australian football, especially the Adelaide Crows) and other stuff.

On the day before we moved to Tasmania, my last day in Adelaide, I bought two packs of the newly released Futera F1 grand prix racing series. In the first pack I opened, I got the winner exchange card, which was one in every 130. I redeemed it and got a specially made card of the winner of the 1995 F1 Adelaide grand prix, the last race held there before it relocated to Melbourne the next year.

I currently have several thousand trading cards in my collection and many of them were from ones I collected way back in the later half of the 1990s. Sometimes I still manage to get a hold of some trading cards to this very day but they are much harder. I did a search on eBay and the majority of the cards are mid-90s, and it demonstrates how the popularity decreased so much until a few years ago. But I think the popularity will eventually pick back up again and I have started seeing more packs of cards in newsagents. I will not sell my collection because if I did, I would not be able to get the money I want, and to get the cards back.

Computer Games

When you are bored there is always a solution to get your brain exercised again, and one of my big lifetime entertainment hobbies were computer or console games; not just playing, but making levels. I started playing Atari 2600 back in 1988 and I used to play Pac Man a lot. I was quite good at it and used to score about 300,000 to 400,000 points until I died out. I cannot remember my true high score. But a couple of years later we got a Sega Master System II and there was a built-in game named Alex Kid In Miracle World. (My mum would have named me Alex if she was awake when I was born.)

It was a side-scrolling platformer, and I used to be able to reach the last level but would always run out of lives, and it was unfair because you got no continues at all. The game would run if you turned on the Sega console with no cartridge in it because it was a built-in game. We gave the Sega Master System to my cousins and bought a NES (Nintendo) and found it much better. My favourite games were Super Mario Bros 2 and 3, popular sideways-scrolling platform games, Batman and Star Wars, which were also both platform games.

I played Super Mario Bros 3 a lot, and every time I lost a life I used to get upset and angry, because losing in anything upset me, and I used to react in a silly way. But as I got better at Super Mario Bros 3, I used to have much more fun with it, and by November 1993 I was able to finish the game and get through it all. I felt like I wasn't so bad at games after all.

By late 1994 I got sick of the NES, and we got a Super NES, and it came with a game named Super Mario All-stars. Super Mario All-stars had Super Mario Bros 1, 2, 3 and the lost levels (Japanese version of SMB2) built into one cartridge. I was absolutely impressed with the differences with the graphics. The music was also pretty cool too, even though the songs were the same. There were distant background hills or clouds which scrolled slower and it looked good. In the cave levels, the sounds and music used to echo, and it sounded like you were in a real cave; even the music sounded like it was getting played in the caves too.

Other games I used to rent were Super Star Wars games, and later on I actually had a copy of the first two games in the Super Star Wars series…both difficult and very challenging games with excellent music.

Then I started renting a game named Doom, a 3D shoot-em-up game I just fell in love with. After playing Wolfenstein 3D on the SNES, I later played Doom and I used to like searching for secret doors, rather than killing enemies, and would end up dead half the time, but when we got a computer a few months later I started playing Doom II early in 1996. The original PC version was the real deal and was tons better than the SNES version; there were floor textures, more enemies, more secrets.

I played and played it for ages and in March 1996 I read in a video game magazine about a Doom level editor where you can make add-on levels for Doom and Doom II, and that got me hooked. In June 1996 I downloaded a Windows-based level editor named DoomCAD. But it was a very hard and frustrating learning experience. It once made me have a tantrum and break the keyboard, a reaction to being overpowered by my point of view.

In July 1996 I made my first-ever working Doom level, two rooms connected to a working door which eventually formed into several rooms with monsters in them. It was an amazing feeling getting that first map working after several failed attempts, possibly due to computer problems and with enemies or monsters running around, but like many people my first levels were awful. I knew there was plenty of room for improvement.

I have created hundreds upon hundreds of levels since 1996 and I'm still designing levels; over 13 years. I even had a Doom add-on web page up on the Internet that I designed myself; you can download my add-ons, including The Twilight Zone, Death Tormention and much more from my own website www.paulcorfiatis.com.

Myself and my friend Kristian from Finland really enjoyed working on a project named Whispers of Satan, which is a full replacement of levels for Doom 2; it took over three years to make. Back in 2000–2002 myself and eight other guys from around the world also worked on a project named 2002 A Doom Odyssey, which is a complete replacement for the original Ultimate Doom. I made 17 of the 36 levels and wrote all the MIDI-based music for this project. I've created several episodes myself. The Twilight Zone and The Twilight Zone 2: Final Dreams are both 32-level episodes created in the late 1990s. I would spend hours a day working on levels, when I was not at school or not playing basketball.

I also worked some more experimental add-ons named Bella and Bella II, which were two episodes for Doom 2 that are more experimental than anything. In 2004 I created a nine-level episode for Doom named Simply Phobos, which concentrates on the style and design of episode one of the Doom game. It was well received by reviewers. I've also worked on several so-called joke episodes, some which haven't impressed some people, and I've gotten a bad reputation in some ways for some time, and that ruined my confidence; I think it was a big mistake.

When I met Kristian, my friend from Helsinki back in 2005 in person, we were at the summer cottage talking about the plans for a new 32-level episode for Doom 2; the plan was for both of us to make 16 levels each.

Late in 2006, work began on the project and I came up with the game Whispers of Satan. Progress was slow because of other things in our lives but we managed to get WOS released on 15 September 2009. It was well reviewed and received a Cacoward (or a Cacodemon award, a Cacodemon being an enemy in Doom and Doom 2) at Doomworld, at the end of the year for its outstanding classic style, design and gameplay.

I also have a secret alter-ego level designer inspired by one of my favourite comedians, Sacha Baron Cohen, the man who acts as Ali G and Borat, who created a series of TV episodes named *Ali G in da USAiii* (aka Da Ali G show) where he goes around interviewing well known people in England and the USA, and trying to fool them with his characters. A new character named Brüno was introduced: a gay Austrian fashion reporter with a mohawk and tight jeans who really did a good job at pissing people off. It was very funny.

So I decided to create my own alter ego or hoax character for the Doom community named Ruba, a fictional ladyboy or shemale from Thailand, heavily inspired by Bruno, mainly because many people out there hate gay people, particularly in the Doom community. Most people are males aged between 15 and 20, and good portions are from the USA, the country of Doom's origin.

Ruba, though gay in his early days, now currently actually has a girlfriend and is not gay himself, but he believes he always wanted to be a woman and decides to get female hormone injections to enlarge breasts, buttocks and remove body hair. Before reading this, nobody at all in the Doom community knew that Ruba was actually me (Paul Corfiatis) and many believe he/she was real. That's exactly what the aim was, because if they found out if it was me I would not have been a very popular person back then.

Ruba in 2009 worked on a 32-level megawad for Doom 2, named Killing Adventure, and received a Cacoward for best comedy WAD of the year, due to its humorous title screen (of a stickman shooting a smiling Cacodemon) and crazy intermission texts. This meant I was the first and probably only person ever, to get two Cacowards in one year. Ruba, though now defunct, released his maps with a very strange design, often with lots of copy and paste and the use of uncharacteristic items, such as Wolfenstein soldiers (which many people hate), Commander Keen dolls, and strange texture choices.

This has led to lots of review abuse, such as 'map made by a fag, avoid 0/5' and other comments showing the negativity of some people.

Ruba's maps often are released with very strange names, resembling those a three-year-old child would mumble, and the descriptions in the text files are often absolutely ridiculous. Ruba's first map ever released was a level named Goomba, the same name used as the Goomba's seen in the Super Mario games which I like playing.

Another early map is called Daffy Uck, which is quite simply Daffy Duck misspelled, since I liked watching cartoons when I was younger. Ruba has uploaded over 50 individual files to the archives, many with strange names, and even though many of the levels are decent (architecture-wise) the item placement and texture usage has generated a decent amount of review abuse, which is exactly how I wanted it to work out. One level named KaKoKa is a blatantly textured map that features Cacodemons (floating redheads) trapped in cages. Hence the name, Kakoka, which is a different spelling for Cacodemon or in other ways Caco.

Some other very strange names used are Wine's Luxury Grange (inspired by rich people drinking wines in stretch limousines), Kastel of the Koberah (Castle of the Cobra), Please get hot jiggi (Jiggy or sexual behaviour in Ali G's terms), Zukky's Gaveyard (graveyard, but spelt more like gay yard, gave or gay), Moggo, Kill the Homies (which can be homeys or homosexuals), Sawun Luajaw Veagiuna (which of course is vagina misspelt), the infamous Kohe series, a series of 15 levels that Ruba made individually and much, much more.

One map named Iraki Terrorist was to simulate the war in Iraq. You are in an outside field where you kill the sergeants and dodge the so called Scud missiles from which a Cyberdemon fires out, with a picture of former USA president George W. Bush behind the Cyberdemon, who can be crushed by pressing a switch on the side of the building, therefore killing Bush (who is of course that Cyberdemon). The aim was to make a very anti-war map, since there are a lot of Americans out there playing these maps, and it's drawn lots of attention, making me happy.

And just to rub more salt into the wounds, the text file of Sawun

Luajaw Veagiuna contains a section Known Bugs: Reviewers to help increase the frequency of review abuse. One of the comments on the archives said this 'From the textfile: Known Bugs: Reviewers. You, Ruba, have to understand that we are not bugs if we hate your crap.' And this really made me laugh. It shows the stupidity of some people in this world, and I think over the last three or four years that the negativity in this world has dramatically increased.

After releasing a level named Connex II (a level with the same room copied and pasted many times), I decided that enough was enough with Ruba, and because of the political chaos in Thailand, Ruba apparently got injured in a gunfight in Bangkok.

The review abuse is a bit like the same thing as Sacha Baron Cohen got spat in his face at times, when he was interviewing people dressed up in his characters, Ali G, and Borat from Kazakhstan, and especially when he was that gay Austrian hooker named Brüno. It is a proof of the sensitivity of panic-stricken people of the modern day.

But I would never do this myself in character in public. After I released my last Ruba project (Killing Adventure, explained before) in 2009, I thought to myself throughout the year to create a new fictional Doom level designer, who makes boring-looking maps with good gameplay, but decided to concentrate more on my own things after work was done on Whispers of Satan.

1996 to 2009 is a very long time and I've dedicated a good portion of my life to this hobby alone. After Whispers of Satan, I made a map named Processing Bunker. It was a haunted, dark underground base level. But my future is to concentrate more on artwork, music, music production, video and sound editing, possible work, and other things that men of course like to do. I'm just like any other male deep in.

Dave, My Alter Ego

I love a laugh, and I love the silliest and childish comedy going around, and have watched a lot of comedians throughout my life, such as Jim Carrey (particularly *Ace Ventura*), Rowan Atkinson (*Mr Bean*) and others. But one that stuck most to me was rapper Ali G, the creation of Sacha Baron Cohen (as explained before), who also is very well known for Borat. I'd love to meet Sacha one day in person, so if you are reading this book, Mr Baron Cohen, I'd love to do an interview with you, or just meet up with you for lunch, because you would be fascinating to talk to.

I based my alter ego on a young teenage girl who flirted with me unsuccessfully. My alter ego is an American dude who, in an absolutely nonsense story, travels to Tasmania in order to find the Tasmanian devil, and his sister, Mary, who was adopted to Tasmania when she was a child, after she shot dead a young woman when she was four years old, by accidentally firing her dad's shotgun. Sounds like an absolutely pointless story. Dave Behringah wears a black, red and white long-sleeved shirt, and a black and red Chicago Bulls 1990s baseball cap facing backwards. He travels around Tasmania in search of the Devil.

I have worked on two 30-minute warm-up episodes, where I, as Dave, interview people and describe some Australian culture, with various sexual spiffs thrown in, particularly when he displays his happiness at being thrown out of high school due to inappropriate behaviour.

One of the people I've interviewed was the daughter of a well known stage actor Lex Marinos; and she is a lovely lady. Her and I planned the interview and Dave asks her out, unsuccessfully, but he high-fives her, happy to find out she has a boyfriend, demonstrating his defensive respect, so he feels good for her. The name Behringah is a misspelling of the name Behringer (a professional audio company based on a surname).

As Dave, I talk with a horrible, loud American accent. Dave explains Aussie rules football, how to steal a car, magic tricks with Blu-tack (the stuff that holds posters on the wall) where Dave divides the balls back and forth, and several failed attempts at other things, to demonstrate how dumb this white American dude is…but in a funny way. The series contains a lot of explicit language and needs to be edited out before I even plan to get it out to TV, and it's unlikely, since some sections also must be removed.

I'd also like to write a short, partially scripted comedy film featuring this character and release it to film festivals. One idea I have for the start of the film is that Dave is having a dream that he walking alone through a quiet forest, and something attacks him, like a ghoul, and Dave awakens and gets out of bed. In reality, myself and a few other friends made that bit of the film – an experimental piece.

Quite possibly, he has three girlfriends wearing colourful bikinis, still asleep beside him and there is no doubt this is an image heavily inspired by some of Ali G's poses with heaps of bikini-clad women.

The aim of the possible movie will be focused on the life of Dave as he continues his search around Tasmania to find the devil, only to find out that there are many devils, since they are a species of animal. Thinking it's the devil from the Loony Tunes cartoons, Dave is disappointed to see that the Devil is a cat-like creature with sharp teeth. I also want to have the scene of a police-car chase, smoking marijuana and bongs, Dave and his friends doing graffiti, and more silly things, such as a scene on his stopover in Bangkok, Thailand, where Dave picks up a hot chick only to find out it's a ladyboy or shemale, and since he has been tricked he isn't impressed at all; he gets angry and tells her to get out of here, or something else more impolite.

Dave is just a hobby, just something I have fun with. Early in 2009, I as Dave Behringah appeared as a host and a guest at the Mad Month of Making at Wynyard, Tasmania. Dave starts an interview with his famous catchphrase 'Yo! Check it out 'n' blow!' I'm also in the planning stages for a Russian alter ego named Vladimir Pretkowski, who is a character similar to Borat, though completely unrelated, and not as rude…but very, very crazy and funny. The plan for Vladimir is to have short hair and a nicely trimmed short length beard, to wear nice clothing, and to speak nice English with an accent.

To get this look, I would have to shave off my hair completely bald with a razor, and shave my face, and let it all grow back for one to two weeks, then trim around the edges of the beard. He does similar things to Dave; interviews people, and goes around talking about various things. He loves children's play equipment and loves playing with little kids to take the mickey out of anti-playful adults.

Facts & Figures

It's a world amongst odds, numbers, patterns and shapes that can give me great pleasure or great displeasure. Is it random or is it rigged? From the odds of finding a special trading card in a pack, to *Deal or No Deal*, a challenging TV game show. Whilst I'm not a big fan of TV game shows, such as *Wheel or Fortune* or the *Price is Right*, I'm a massive fan of *Deal or No Deal* because of the odds, risks and challenge.

You get 26 cases containing 26 different amounts up to $200,000; you pick one case, which is your case, and then you pick six, five, four, three, two, then one case at a time and you're offered what's available after each round. Say 'Deal', and you win this amount of cash; say 'No deal' and you must proceed with a risk of eliminating big amounts.

I figure out that men are much more risk-takers than women, though I have seen women go for gold.

Some people are lucky, and others are unlucky, and that could be perhaps me some day as a contestant, doing some deals and facing a challenge to win some cash.

In 2008 and 2009 I compiled all the results of *Deal or No Deal* episodes aired on TV, to see what the odds are. The stats for *Deal or No Deal* have been published on my website (www.paulcorfiatis.com) For example, briefcases two, 12, 19, 20 or 21 are more likely to contain a $20x,xxx amount, but can still contain anything else at any other time.

I hate losing, and I always love a challenge in life. It's very disappointing to see somebody risk a large amount of cash and leave with very little, while it's a fantastic feeling when somebody wins a large amount of cash.

It's amazing all the greedy people and risk-takers you get on the show. While some are lucky, many aren't so lucky, and that's how it goes.

One contestant in 2007 looked like he was in tears after he refused to take a $37,000 offer. For several years I used to buy lotto tickets, but the most I ever won was about $50, and sometimes I play keno, and I've won over $100 during one occasion. For several years I used to compile the Saturday lotto results and, from what I've figured out, there seemed to be a higher amount division one winners when there were several closely spaced numbers, like 4, 7, 8, 11, 32, 35 for example.

Maybe I should enter these previous numbers onto a ticket, and maybe I could be a very lucky person. Highly spread numbers tends to produce fewer winners. Eight balls are drawn in Saturday lotto here in Australia, six winning numbers and two supplementary numbers, so if you get all six winning numbers correct, you share for example, $4 million with four winners. So you get $1 million, and by today's standards that is not a huge amount of money. The average house costs 40% of that amount alone, and it's certainly not enough these days to buy a dream mansion overlooking the beach on the Gold Coast. One of our friends here in Ulverstone won the Saturday lotto division one, and I started losing interest after that, as I was spending $20 a week with little or no luck, so I quit, and only put on occasional tickets.

When I was collecting trading cards when I was younger, back in the mid to late 1990s, I certainly enjoyed the challenge. For example, a trading card series contains a main set of, let's say, 200 cards. These are called common cards, but randomly inserted into the packs were the insert or chase cards. For example, one insert set has 15 cards and is one in every four packs (or packets or wrappers or whatever), while something rare is one in every 100 packs. I loved this challenge and sometimes I pulled something hard to find out of the packet. My best was a card that was inserted into one in every 128 packs. I purchased just two packets, and that was the first card I saw. It still sits in my folder redeemed.

As you know, I also like the facts and figures of aircraft, registrations and other types of transport, such as the consists of trains for example, which railcar I have been on before, and all that stuff. And of course the facts and figures of space and astronomy, the masses of each planet and moon for example.

Musical Experience

From a young child I knew I could write music. I used to bang on the cupboards and use them as a percussion instrument, and record them on to cassette; and I used to hum stuff out of my mouth…but the technology wasn't that great back then.

Fast forwarding to the late 1990s after we moved to Tasmania, we started getting computers and I fell in love with the shoot-em-up game Doom, and particularly its add-on levels (or wad files). Some of the add-on packs for Doom and Doom 2 I have downloaded from the net had new music in them.

I knew that a lot of this music was written from scratch, especially for the add-on, and I started wondering, because I knew I had the ability to write my own music. I played another Doom-like game, named Hexen. It had some real great music, but that music was on the CD as tracks and I started finding out that it was the sound from a Roland device.

My worker Steve bought his own computer and he got Cakewalk Home Studio, a program which enables you to write your own midi files from scratch and mix down music. You have 16 different channels where you can put your instrument in. Channel 10 was the drum track. There is also a list of 120-weight different instruments ranging from pianos, guitars, and orchestral instruments.

The first song I ever wrote, named 'Life after Death', was in November 1998. It was a medieval theme and Hexen inspired me to write that song. So I used medieval orchestral instruments like string ensembles, timpani drums. A lot of my early songs used instrument patches in the 127-patch general midi, with strange names like Banjo (Silly Country Music), Agogo, Kalimba (Sounded African to me) and Bagpipe (of course Scottish).

I knew what a bagpipe and banjo were, but what the heck was

an agogo timpani or kalimba like? I later found out an agogo was a type of percussive bell, actually two cone-sized cowbells which hang off a washing line, or anything a bit like that, and you tap it with anything. I found out that the timpani are actually a set of several drums used in orchestras which can be tuned separately into different pitches. I actually started remembering how I played timpani drums in Grade 9 class band before I even was interested in writing music on my computer. The teacher called them kettledrums.

But the sounds of the instruments on my computer didn't sound right; they sounded a bit like digitised Atari-like beeps, because of the low-quality midi interface in the sound card.

So I saved up and bought myself a Yamaha XG soft synthesiser which adds much more realistic-sounding midi instruments to your computer. I started writing my own dance-like techno music and I have made a few copies on CDs. I wanted to name the album *Power Zone* but my worker Steve said I should give it another name because I might be stealing a trademark. So I named it *EuXoia*, which is a very strange name indeed.

My favourite types of music are anything different. When I first heard electronic rap music in about 1988 on the FM radio it blew me away. The name of the group was Technotronics. Their song 'Pump up the Jam' was a number one hit back then when I was little. I used to listen to lots of music on the radio. I wanted a copy of their tape (album) then but I never got one.

I used to like anything which pumped out the speakers. Bob Marley's reggae music sounded good, and I liked the sound of his wild voice, the kick drum, piano, double bass, cowbells and steel drums. I really liked Kodo, a Japanese taiko drumming ensemble. My favourite taiko drumming tracks by Kodo are 'Lion', 'Miyake', 'O-Daiko', 'Monochrome', 'Irodori', 'Zoku' and 'Chonlima'. Anything which has a ferocious drumming action with superbly timed beats and drumming patterns (and production of the recording such as panning) makes me feel awake and lively.

I also like orchestras, and I like the composition by Gustav Holst named *The Planets*. I like 'Jupiter' and 'Uranus' because they are both very dramatic and have a lot of use of timpani drums; I also like anything else dramatic like the *Star Wars* title theme and the *Empire Strikes Back* imperial march theme.

I also go to see our Tasmanian symphony orchestra (TSO) live. I saw three TSO performances in 2000. In May I drove my car from Ulverstone to Launceston and back with my support worker. Then I saw them perform in Burnie Civic Centre in October, and that was my favourite, because it had very good seating. And in December I saw them play at Town Hall in Devonport. I spent most of my time staring at the timpani player in the percussion section, as he sometimes beat the buggery out of those drums. I also like bagpipes too, especially when 'Scotland the Brave' or 'Bonnie Dundee' is played through them.

After composing mainly midi files from 1998 to 2000, in late 2000 I was introduced to a professional recording studio in Burnie, where I started to learn music and audio editing the professional way. Throughout 2001 I started working on many various experimental songs using combined audio and midi. Most of the songs were dance or house songs and decided to name this new generation Dripper.

As I got better I released three private independent Dripper albums. In July 2004 I put out *Dripper – Into a Dark Era* and have sold plenty of copies, and that was followed up with *Dripper – D-Metl* and *Dripper – Hyperactive*, which were released in smaller quantities. Most of the songs on these compilations combine an experimental and personal (from my point of view) style of house and trance music, with a mixture of drum loops and synths, and synth basses.

All of this is done in the computer, and you have separate tracks; some midi and some audio, and you can adjust the volume levels, or panning of each track to get the right sound.

In 2005 I was extremely depressed; in *Dripper – Hyperactive* I started working on a new style unlike the first two recordings. This genre I was aiming at was Psychedelic Trance, under inspiration from my best friend in Finland, who I've known for many years. And during this down time in my life I never felt so inspired when it comes to writing music.

The album was completed early in 2006 and several copies were printed and mainly sold to friends, like the first two albums for example. Midway through 2006, I started working on a new series of 20 trance and psytrance songs and one chill-out song, under the artist name of Nemrac, which I thought at one stage changing to NemRack for better pronunciation. The series is expected to be completed in 2008 and played in live sets in the future, as my confidence and self-esteem is vastly growing. This new series of music is my best ever and I'm planning in getting it released in Europe and other countries where the genre is popular. Psychedelic drugs are popular such as magic mushrooms, LSD and Ecstasy at these psytrance events, but I don't plan on taking any of them due to a lack of interest.

I also earned some money by writing jingles and have already sold dozens of them for radio and airplay.

Midway through 2006 I was assigned to work on a 5.1 soundtrack for a Tasmanian Big Hart Radio Holiday project, and I put together 12 x 5.1 surround sound tracks which were played at Melbourne's Federation Square in October 2006. I flew over to Melbourne for a few days to witness this, and spent a lot of time checking out the place. The money that I earned went towards paying off my car and I had to start saving up all over again roughly, as I aimed to travel overseas in 2007, but I couldn't achieve that goal due to other personal reasons.

Despite suffering depression from time to time, I continued to work on my Nemrac series into 2008, and each song is very different from the other, particularly one song (the 15th in the series) named Trylobyte, which contains a superb recreation of the Scottish bagpipes using a TS404 Soft Synth.

When we moved to another home in January 2008, I added a small entry-level home studio to my set-up, a pair of good-sounding studio monitor speakers and a mix console, but I will eventually upgrade it to a better set-up when I get the funds. This will include external synths, better studio speakers and an appropriate location; plus, also gain more exposure to playing live sets, because I know it will be an enjoyable hobby. The sky is the limit.

At the end of 2008 the series had reached 20 songs, 19 trance songs and one chill-out song, but at any possible planned gigs in the future I will only play a random assortment of the songs, along with my older Dripper songs.

Outside of my own music I was involved in a few more projects for Big Hart, 'This is Living' and 'Love Zombies', with me remixing older-style music into more modern pieces, and also doing lots of photography for our shows. My work experiences will be explained later on.

I also have been doing casual mixing and production work with a local artist named Simon Cazaly at the recording studio, and we've become very good mates over the years. We've recorded and mixed down three albums from 2002 to 2009 with a total of about 35 songs.

Modern Living

The Biggest Test of All

From 2001 to 2004 I was lonely, and totally out of phase, and was suffering from quite a bit of depression. I thought to myself that the next few years were going to be a huge test for me.

A lot of my time was dedicated to my fitness, work with music and at home. But I knew I could get more social, and I met quite a few interesting people along the way of the right and wrong types. I continued to struggle with girls at times because of my anxiety, and it's not funny at all!

I aimed for more male friends, since I felt more comfortable around them, and then met some female friends along the way. But some friends seem to just pretend, a few would completely ignore my text messages, and even though they were nice to me, it made me feel very worried, and rejected. Some bad experiences I have had in the past makes me feel uncomfortable with certain people. High school years were very tough and I felt much rejected, especially by some of the girls.

I decided to get off my butt and start meeting new people in the upcoming years and I succeeded with some very good friends, and some not so good friends.

In September 2004 I met a guy named Telen (his name used with permission). He was well worth meeting because if I did not ever meet him things just would have not been right. Telen has a lot of hobbies and he is quite an active person; he is into movie and music making, and works for NWRSS (North West Residential Support Services: Wynyard) and Big Hart. Through him I have met quite a lot of other people and have made some good friends.

Myself and Telen have spent countless hours talking about good and bad things, and we have been out, and done a lot of things together. We have been to Melbourne, we have been to movies, night clubs, theatre and much more. We have had our opportunity to perform our own music to the public. Meeting Telen has made my day. He is a very physical person who likes the challenge of many things, and me writing this in here will make him feel proud.

I returned to Adelaide by myself in late March 2007 and the trip was a great success; to be able to travel all on my own, change planes by myself, and more. I caught up with mainly family and friends and went to see an AFL game. In fact, it was the sixth time I saw a game live featuring the Adelaide Crows (including a few in Launceston).

I snapped a lot of aircraft photos at Adelaide and Melbourne airports during the trip, of which many have been uploaded to the Internet. I also made a return trip to Adelaide a few months later for my grandmother's 70th, which was a much better trip than the first. Another trip followed in March 2008, just after that infamous heatwave.

Telen and I have been involved in several projects with Big Hart, including Love Zombies, This is Living, Mad Month of Making, Drive and NWRSS…such as a trip down to Hobart in part of a video project. I've also met many other people in Burnie and through Big Hart, so I have to credit myself with my achievements in improving my social life.

Originally my manners were not that good (due to my impatience) but self-belief has improved my manners over the years, and I think there is always more room for improvement. Later in 2009 it felt like I was being left again out when everybody ignored my text messages, when I was trying to plan things for New Year's Eve, and I'm thinking, have they given up on me?

It's very, very frustrating when you have to do it on your own, and that's one thing I need to adjust to. I met a really cool guy later in 2009 and we get on very well and we have done some music mixing together.

Family Business

This section is all about today's living at home (or as I could say, more like living at home in the recent past) and describing how I have grown into myself as of today. Living is expensive today, as we all know, with me from a working-class family. My father is foreign and was in and out of jobs, and now is on a pension.

Though my mother is special, she has bought me up from a chipmunk into a champmunk; or in proper English, I could say she has made me grow from that little boy into a mature adult. My dad at times can be a bit stressful, since he has a loud voice and I often find people like that very stressful, because I feel like I have been overpowered. My brother is similar to my father. He loves fast cars, and can be quite hard on me, but these days I often just take it, since I've grown up…and I just keep my distance.

But several years ago things did get a bit unstable and I would eventually lose patience. There was one day I was watching AFL football and I was yelling at the TV, and then my mum and brother butt in, and start giving me hell. I tell them to stop, but they continue; so I lose my patience and walk out the back door and slam it.

My bro as I said before loves fast cars, particularly Mazdas and Nissans. He had this old Mazda sedan, then he had a Holden VL Commodore in perfect condition and the car got written off after only a few months due to suffering severe rear-end damage. Then he gets a loan for a really nice Nissan 200SX twin turbo. I hope, for dear lord, he can actually start understanding that a car is not a toy, because I treat cars good. I don't go crazy with them.

He has had a few jobs and I hope he always does well. At other times he can be really nice. When my parents were away in Launceston (Dad had a big operation for prostate cancer) after I came home one night, we actually had a real good talk about our problems, so there are good times as well.

But after that he is his usual self, good 70% of the time, frustrating the other 30% of the time, and that makes it tough living at home.

The problem that is preventing me from moving is the lack of money. I don't have any proper work, since full-time casual jobs aren't my thing, but I have gotten some paid work at the recording studio, and worked on a soundtrack for a Melbourne festival and also written jingles for TV and radio ads. The problem is I spend the money.

I am slowly assembling my home theatre system at the time of writing; all I need is the TV, DVD player and a subwoofer, and I'm planning on starting to build my own home studio. The surround sound amp and speakers are connected to my computer but in 2008 I bought a cheap subwoofer, painted it and added it to complete the system, then bought a lovely set of VAF speakers in June 2009 which I use for music listening and some monitoring.

As I said, life at home is frustrating at times, but great at other times. Moving out of home would be an excellent choice for me in the future. Several times I've lived in a unit in Wynyard, Tasmania, and certainly enjoyed living there on my own. But if I rented, there are problems, such as bills, and that prevents you from saving up as much as you living at home for example.

I'm planning on going on at least one more overseas trip before I get out of home, possibly to Finland again, but I'd love to go to Thailand, Singapore, the USA and several other countries. I set myself a goal to move out of home. My original plan was when I turned 27 I'm out of the house during that year, no matter what, but then again, other things might delay my move, which is exactly what happened.

As explained just before, late in 2008 and early 2009 I lived on my own in Wynyard during three separate stints for a few weeks during a project, and I enjoyed the peace and quiet; and I lived in Wynyard later in 2009 for the Drive project. This is thanks to Neal and Pam, my good friends, whose unit it is.

Humans are territorial animals and they are intelligent, and they want certain things, like money, and this keeps them happy. Some families don't have much money at all.

Another possibility is perhaps moving to mainland Australia might help me increase my chances in getting exposure to my music, and besides most of my good friends are in Adelaide. I'm the one that left them behind.

Moving away from Adelaide just before my 14th birthday was like having to start life all over again once in Tasmania, but of course over time I've adjusted, despite many challenges. In January 2008 we moved to another home and things seem vastly more settled and improved. My brother has improved a lot, and is more grown up, and I feel somewhat more comfortable in the newer house.

Sometimes I watch something exciting on the TV like *Deal or No Deal* or the AFL football, and my brother often storms into my room in a state where he wants to smash my nose in. He never does. Mum says my screaming at the TV annoys him. I find that extremely annoying, and Dad often gets involved to make things worse. Not fun at all. But as the year progressed I learnt to keep cooler.

My brother took a big step in his life when he moved to up Queensland later in the year and found a job; so I'm pleased for him. But he eventually returned home to live with us and he is doing pretty well, and he has been much more manageable throughout 2009; a good thing for sure.

Another problem living in this house is that we are not allowed to have pets, but almost all the time there is at least one cat in our front or backyard, three cats next door and a family of cats from further up the road. The brownish grey female tabby cat is always on the run for food because of her kittens, and her long-haired tortoiseshell sister sits in a box by our back door. Several kittens have visited.

It's kind of crazy with all these cats, especially with my mum being a cat lover. We eventually gave away all these cats and kittens, so they now have good homes, except for one of the cats. But despite giving them away, more cats have visited. A black and white calico tortoiseshell from next door has decided to move in with a nice big orange tabby (the brother) visiting quite often. There is no escape from these hairy friends, or shall I say hairy creatures that rub all over your legs. It kind of tickles when you don't expect it, and it's like 'Oh, what's that?'

I often now have dinner in my bedroom because I hate the TV

commercials and my parents don't like me muting the TV when the commercial break comes on. I do this mainly because of some of the music in these commercials.

Girlfriends Good & Bad

After some early struggles, I met my first girlfriend at high school in 1998 when I was 16. She was slightly older than me and I found her fairly easy going and open, and we saw each other a few times a week. But a few years later we disagreed with certain things and just decided to be good old friends; so it didn't really matter if she got another boyfriend (which she did eventually get, also with high functioning autism). We continued to see each other for a few more years before things faded back.

I also met a few various people early in the 2000s but I cost myself with anxiety. I also met a rather interesting person who was an immigrant from former Yugoslavia (Serbia and Montenegro) but I got really anxious and said a few things I probably should have not said; but we still had our good times.

It was probably a fear of things after a girl at high school tricked me in a way that she was single, but was actually seeing somebody. I got upset with her and yelled at her one day. And then as I walked away from her she threw a glass bottle in the back of my head and I reacted by turning back at her, and threw myself on to her. I had no intention to injure her and there were no injuries. It was not a nice experience to be honest, but I apologised to her later in the week and moved on. But I think this has affected me in some ways, especially with my confidence.

When I went to Hellyer College in Burnie in 2000 I met a few other girls; one of them had Down's syndrome but she was a really sweet person. I saw her for only a few months, and on and off over the years, but her mother was protective. There was also another girl I saw for a few weeks, just for some fun and nothing serious.

But yet again back then, my anxiety and fear or rejection stopped me from trying and I had thoughts of oh, every good-lookin' chick has a boyfriend, or does she have a boyfriend, should I ask her out? for example.

After leaving school, the next few years were fairly quiet and I didn't really bother with anybody, apart from an Internet pen pal who I still know to this very day, but haven't met. I did come close to meeting her in 2002, but lost my chance.

My brother met somebody very decent in 2003 and spent just over two years with her. This person had a much younger sister who was quite mature and grown up (like a woman); surely she was sixteen, not twelve. Halfway through 2005 something between us started to form, and I thought, oh a nice pretty girl who likes me, and once I noticed that I did the wrong thing by reacting to her, and that I shouldn't have felt like that. I was 23 at the time, and she was 13 (four years under the age of consent) and I should have ignored her. It was hard because of my mental sickness and depression, but I thought to myself this can't happen to me, and my only solution was to complain to her mother. She was following me around and she lied about me, and I got accused of liking her, for all the wrong reasons.

Much as I would have, I didn't want to make love to her because of the law; because I wanted to spend my life outside of jail. This was shortly before my trip to Finland to see my overseas pen pal. I was freaked out by this girl and didn't go into town after school for several months (until November) and guess what, this girl and her friends ambushed me, and I just sat there thinking it was all a joke. They wanted me to come with them but I just refused. I realised they were playing a game.

A few months later I went for a swim at the beach, and guess who got in the water with me…it's kinda funny. Things have settled down since and this girl, 10 years younger than me, was probably the turning point in my life, which cured the terrible depression I suffered in 2005 mainly because of loneliness and fear of rejection.

But things started to slowly improve over the forthcoming years.

Early in 2006 I met a fairly nice lady and we saw each other on and off for the next three and a half years. She was over 12 years older than me but very pretty, attractive and smart, and we had lots of interesting conversations. But we also had some low times as well because she suffered from mental sickness as well.

Our relationship ended in October 2009 when she had a sore leg injured in a balcony collapse at her house. I had taken her home from hospital, and tried to be supportive. She asked me to look for a key ring, but I had no clue where it was located within her messy house, and because she was screaming and yelling at me not to touch her things, I replied (yelled), 'Now how do you expect me to find things, if you don't want me touching your things?' – my temper boiled over and I yelled and kicked the plasterboard hallway wall in, and stormed out the door. It was the longest drive back home, trust me.

I was devastated but happy the next day that I made the decision not to see her any more, but I was also thinking, oh I was getting better and I took a step back with my lost temper, and considered this a failure; but at the same time couldn't handle all this yelling and screaming from her. It really irritated me.

With upcoming work I needed more time by myself. Early in 2009 I had this fairly nice girlfriend; it was a short-lived relationship. We just unfortunately didn't match. Life sucks sometimes. Later in 2009 I met this very nice and friendly lady, but she plans to move overseas…I can't win. I met an Internet friend in 2010, a person I first chatted to online way back in 1999–2001 and have met her a few times face to face, and we had a lot in common, but it's never easy when they live far away. And what upset me is that two weeks after I met her, she met another guy.

Now I regret not meeting her back in 2000; all because of my shyness…it was terrible. I thought I had found the perfect future girlfriend but we will keep in touch hopefully. The disappointment was huge, because it feels that my luck is just terrible and it gets harder and harder every time. I got on well with this person because she has an autistic son, so I found it fascinating to talk to her. We will keep in touch as friends. But I will progress with my life and do what I have to do.

I also wasted a few chances with a few more people. One person I met who was visiting Wynyard planned to go out with me for the day, but before this could happen, she was called back to Hobart for work. So the possibility is that she'll find somebody else; which is exactly what happened.

I had a chance with another person from Burnie, but she found somebody and moved down to Hobart. Once again I missed my chance in not trying hard enough, due to fear of rejection. But with so many relationships breaking up today, due to increased negativity in this world, I'm sure I will get another chance. But it would have to be with the right person.

But meeting a complete stranger one-on-one is not easy, so why do I bother trying? I don't want negativity in my life any more, because I've been through too much of it in the past. So remember, I do not spend all day thinking about this, because it's best not to think about this topic, and do what you need to do most, which is more important to you.

Trip To Finland August 2005

In 1999 I downloaded an add-on for the computer game Doom 2 which was created by a Finnish author, and was impressed. I decided to contact him and invited him to see if he wanted to start working with add-on episodes with me. He agreed to join in with the fun and we worked on a few add-on packs. But what got me keen about him was he started writing his own electronic music.

He had to go into the army but we still kept in touch, and midway through 2004 I announced to him in an Internet chat that I wanted to go to Helsinki to meet him. Over the years leading up to this trip we had worked on various projects together. And we also spent many months chatting about various and funny things, and early in 2005 I obtained my Australian passport, as I was saving up for the trip. After six months of saving up I had booked my ticket to Helsinki, along with my mum, who was organised to go along with me as the support worker.

On 21 August we began our trip, flying out of Devonport on a Qantaslink Dash 8 Q300 regional aircraft during the afternoon to Melbourne. We enjoyed a sunset on this flight on the noisy little plane, before getting to Melbourne and waiting about four hours. At 11.30 that night we departed on a Qantas Airbus A330-300 to Hong Kong. The flight on this very quiet but jam-packed aircraft lasted for about nine hours. It was so quiet that I managed about three or four hours of sleep, and we were greeted by a spectacular tropical dawn at cruising altitude.

I was sitting in the aisle seat in the middle of the plane but could still see outside the window, which had its shutter or blind open. When we got to Hong Kong International the following morning, the sun was already above the horizon. The weather was partially cloudy, misty and warm (and very humid, but not hot) being in August. The airport was surrounded by some enormous hills covered completely by mysterious dense forest. The pollution was high too; many industrial areas and factories were seen. But this was a one-off stop on the trip, and as we waited several hours the sun got higher into the sky. We eventually boarded our flight to Helsinki after a few hours wait on a Finnair MD-11 for a 10-hour flight across Asia.

The plane was nice and comfortable with good leg room, and the flight took us over China, Mongolia, Russia, Kazakhstan (no Borat there, unfortunately; he's just fictional) and a few other places. We flew north of Moscow as well. I was exceptionally lucky as I had a window seat, but my views were ruined by annoying cloudy weather, especially over China, which was going through its wet season. The weather was mostly cloudy those regions.

We arrived in Helsinki on 22 August during a dull, cool but very humid cloudy Monday afternoon, and I met my friend face to face after more than 24 hours in flight. It was rather confusing because there were hundreds of people at the airport holding up signs with people's surnames, but we found them, and my goal was reached.

It was a rather cloudy afternoon in Helsinki and we drove back to his home and settled in. Later we went for a walk together, laughing and joking about the things we liked. I was quite shy for a couple of days and it was a bit too much.

This trip was highly successful. After a good night's sleep myself and my buddy went off into Helsinki and we saw some real ancient buildings, and I must say it was such a different but amazing place. We went across to an island on a ferry to an old medieval castle gardens complex; some which was destroyed. There were some homes on this island in which we were not allowed in. We found old cannons, and old submarine which we were allowed in.

My mate really liked the young lady inside that submarine, and told me. After several hours of exploring this ancient building site, we went back downtown and had some drinks atop of a rather tallish building, which presented us some big views of the city. Then we took ourselves back to the metro (underground/open air suburban train) and went back home. After a long day, we were worn exhausted with about five or six hours non-stop walking in the warm conditions.

We went back home and worked on our Doom add-on project together in the evening, an add-on named Death Tormention 3, which was released later in the year. I worked on E4M5 (Episode 4, Mission 5) for the project, and I had never felt so inspired before, when doing something like this sitting next to this guy; we only previously emailed to each other for many years.

We went out to some nightclubs and they were all an enjoyable experience, and went to the movies, or theatre, to see some real good Batman movie. I got to meet some of my friend's local friends, and his brother who was in the army at the time.

We stopped in Turku and a few other towns like Porvuu along our way to a summer cottage, which was located out in an island in a remote area, and I must say it was a very relaxing place away from everything. The only problems were the mosquitoes, out in their hundreds.

Myself and my friend also had a few arguments over disagreeing with a few things, but I was also recovering from some mental sickness, and I got a bit upset at him, but we solved our problem and our last few days were very good.

We flew back home safely early in September, returning on another Finnair MD-11 to Singapore, stopping at Bangkok – a place I'd like to visit in the future, mainly because it's a city like a challenging video game…the heat, pollution and different people. On this flight we witnessed a spectacular sunrise outside the window even though I had no window seat.

We changed to Qantas in Singapore, on a Boeing 747-400, and flew back to Melbourne. Just before we got to Melbourne we flew over Adelaide at 39,000 feet in the early hours of the morning, and we saw the entire suburban area lit up at night, since I was able to look out the window of the rear door.

We were back in Devonport at 10 a.m. after flying on a QantasLink Dash 8-100 or perhaps 200, and it was sort of very strange getting back home again. I stared out the window watching the plane's shadow as it transited amongst the clouds. But I was happy in many ways to be home after this rather spectacular overseas trip. I had a sore throat and I was very fatigued for a week or so, but recovered well and was playing basketball a couple of weeks later.

It was a big achievement for me meeting this person, and I learnt a lot from him, and this made me grow bigger and better after I was suffering badly from mental problems in the months leading up to the trip. All because of a silly little girl who was playing around with me, and I didn't know what to think, say or do.

I plan to go back to Finland again sometime in the future.

Work

Saving up isn't that easy, and for many years I have been living on the disability pension. But I've had a bit of work experience in 2004 and 2005. Firstly at a CD shop, which went excellent, but I wasn't prepared to work on my own. Secondly, at a print and design place, which went very good but they had no positions vacant, and thirdly, two days of work experience at the Harvey Norman store in Ulverstone. This went well until it failed miserably due to a staff member who verbally abused me, and I just walked out without letting anyone know a thing. Even worse, I hurt my knee later on that day.

Due to my talents and abilities I've been employed by a company named Big Hart Inc since 2006, thanks to that guy named Telen I met a few years ago; he has helped me dearly. I've been involved in several projects, the first was composing a three-hour-long ambient soundtrack for Radio Holiday, an event held in Melbourne and north-west Tasmania. Then late in 2007 I did some music work for a stage play named *This is Living*.

But the best of them all was working on some of the music for another play named *Love Zombies* at Wynyard High School in Tasmania. I became pretty well known by a lot of the students during this time, and all our shows went pretty good.

Most of the work I've been given is remixing 1960s–1970s pieces into more modern techno or trance music; not a fun thing to do, because I have to adjust the speed of these songs and make them faster, so loops can fit in.

Early in 2009 I was involved in a project named The Mad Month of Making which was held in Wynyard, where we had a skateboarding half-pipe set up under a large tree. A good thing, because of the weather on some of the days was quite warm. For this project I did a bit of music work, but also introduced a bit of acting as well, especially as my alter ego character Dave Behringah.

It was challenging, I must admit, but enjoyable too. We also had a week of hard musical work at the studio during one week in September, where I had to produce and mix down a few of the songs for this project. It was very demanding but well worth it in the end. I also have casual work at the recording studio with an artist named Si Cazaly for over half a dozen years, which earns me gradual payouts.

We've just finished a third album together. Later in 2009 I was involved in another Big Hart project named Drive, and I worked on soundscapes at the recording studio, did some video editing for the website, and some mixing at the studio in 2008, as explained before.

It was a rather challenging job but I have enjoyed it 95% of the time, mainly due to the social side of things. All this work decreased my creativity because I found it hard to concentrate on too may things at once, but I go out and do it. But my brain tends to operate on one project better than two or three projects at once.

I worked out at Wynyard from mid-October until just before Christmas. *Drive* is a documentary shown on national TV about young guys, cars, alcohol, rev heads. There are some sad stories in this film, I must admit. But it's all true, it's no lie.

Future Dreams

One thing I'm looking forward to doing in the future is moving into a home of my own, since living at home is not all that enjoyable anymore. But at least it still gives me a roof over my head. The goal is to save up enough money while living at home so I can buy several items; and work opportunities among other things should help me save up over the next few years.

But one day, assuming that I have the money, I'd love to get a house of my own layout built, which will contain features such as an indoor gym for basketball and working out (assuming that I'm not too old), a personal recording studio and a dedicated home cinema or stereo system listening room, with high-quality speakers and large television. The house also has to have the usual features, at least three bedrooms and so on since I could have my own kids with a person that I could meet (who I could trust) someday. I can picture the house near the beach or in the hills amongst the countryside.

I would also like to travel overseas to various destinations and explore this world every person lives on. As a child I had a dream where I could travel into space, and perhaps set foot on Mars, and this is still a possibility in my lifetime depending on costs, and if the political system all works out for itself. But it's 2009, and I think people can get to Mars in the next 10 years only if they stop wasting their money on weapons and useless things. Once I'm dead I do not want to be buried; instead, I want to get my ashes sent out of the solar system in a capsule because I feel like I want to be a great explorer into many places where mankind is not likely to venture for a very, very long time.

So please cremate me, and send me to Gliese 581, Tau Ceti, Aldebaran… I'll decide for sure if or when that day approaches.

Thanks for taking your time to read this book and going on an adventure through my autistic world, venturing through my challenges. I know I am the person that I am. The way nature created me is the way I turned out to be.

Not many autistic people are capable of writing a whole book about themselves; few have done it, even though I feel like now I'm currently a normal person. From all my experiences and reactions, try and compare them to you. I've written as much I could have explained, but I know I could have written more.

I wrote the original draft for this book in November 2000 and it was only about 20% of its current length. It's kinda funny how it took over nine years to make and I probably spent a total of three months working on it. It's a journey over the years; my ups and downs, and with all of my Doom level designing, writing music, basketball, surfing the Internet, and so on, and so forth. Believe it or not, it's kinda crazy.